Sailors Surprised

First published in 2015 by Nigel Reed of Topsails.co.uk
Upside, Loe Beach, Feock Cornwall TR3 6SH
ISBN 978-0-9934322-2-4
Copyright © belongs to Nigel Reed
Illustration copyright © Yuki Reed, Nigel Reed and Colin Pritchard

Printed in Cornwall by Mid Cornwall Printing Truro TR1 2ST

Let's meet Kevin and his friends in Boatland

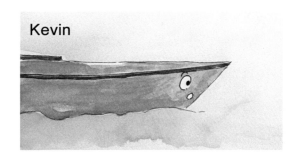

Kevin

Kevin the Canvas Canoe is quick thinking and agile. He tends to lead the boats into action. He has explored the Summerwater for many years and knows its hidden secret places.

Tim the Tender is a small boat who spends a lot of his Summer helping the sailors to go out to their bigger boats kept on the moorings. Because of his size he has to be careful not to be hurt by big waves.

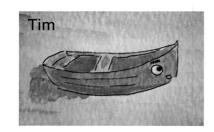

Tim

Yasmin

Marmaduke the Motor Cruiser is thought to be an important boat. He can be a little pompous, but he has a strong sense of duty and likes helping as part of the team.

Yasmin the Yacht is a fine looking craft with a tall slender mast and sleek lines down her blue and white hull. She likes adventures and is kind to her friends.

Marmaduke

Willie the Working Boat spends a lot of the Winter dredging for oysters. Willie has lived in the Summerwater for many a long year and is a little old fashioned in his ways. He prefers to use his red and white sails than his new engine for example.

Willie

Robert the Racing Dinghy is a sporty boat, who enjoys speed and fun. Robert can be impatient and likes to get things done fast. He races every weekend.

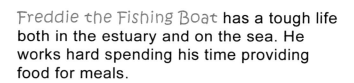
Robert

Tom the Tug is very strong, and too large to live with the other boats at Sandybanks beach. He lives in Bigport docks, but likes joining the other boats in their adventures. He has a no-nonsense approach to life, and uses his strength for good purposes.

Tom
Freddie

Freddie the Fishing Boat has a tough life both in the estuary and on the sea. He works hard spending his time providing food for meals.

An introduction to the Summerwater.

In the far South West of Boatland, there is a beautiful estuary called the Summerwater. At the North end, there is a beach called Sandybanks, where Kevin the Canvas Canoe and his boat-friends live on the water.

Not far from Sandybanks beach, there is a village pub called the Anchor and Keg.

It is a small old pub with a thatched roof. On sunny warm days its customers often sit outside to drink and chat in the sunshine in a garden.

Inside it has black oak beams running across the ceilings and in the winter it always has a large roaring log fire.

It is not the sort of place where you expect trouble to happen...........................

It was one dark, cold, winter evening, on a Friday in December. In the boat yard behind Sandybanks beach, Kevin the Canvas Canoe and his friends were sleeping under the moon.

Friends in the picture opposite:-

Marmaduke the Motor Cruiser
Yasmin the Yacht
Willie the Working Boat
Robert the Racing Dinghy

Kevin the Canvas Canoe
Tim the Tender

They were suddenly awakened by loud noises coming from the Anchor and Keg inn. The front door had burst open, letting a shaft of light out, all the way down to the boatyard.
Three drunken sailors tumbled out of the pub. They were shouting all sorts of rude things about the pub landlord.

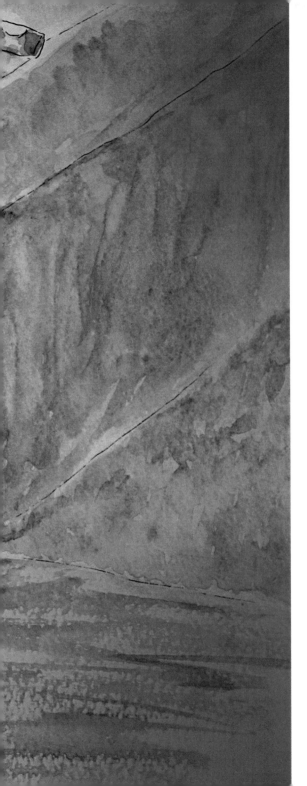

Kevin, who was now wide awake, thought to himself – They don't seem to be a nice bunch of sailors; there could be trouble coming.
And sure enough there was.

The sailors were staggering down the path from the pub, kicking at things as they went. They were not thinking about the damage they might do. One kicked over a statue of an elf at the edge of old Mrs White's garden and another threw a bottle into the hedge.
 "Not nice people at all," thought Kevin.

By then, all six boats, Kevin, Tim the Tender, Marmaduke the Motor Cruiser, Yasmin the Yacht, Willie the Working Boat and Robert the Racing Dinghy had been woken up. Tim, who was the smallest, was frightened by the sailors.

As they went past Tim, next to the rack, one lashed out with his boot and caught him amidships – that is a nautical expression for in the middle.

Tim gasped with the pain.

But before the boats could react, the drunken sailors had run down Sandybanks pontoon and sped away in a motor boat.

"Are you alright, Tim?" said Kevin.
There was no reply.

"Tim" - said Yasmin "do tell us you are alright."
There was a small groan as Tim tried to reply.
"Yes" croaked Tim, who obviously meant No, but Tim was trying to be brave.
"What happened?" asked Robert. "Have they hurt you?
"Ooooh, I think they have cracked one of my gunnels." said Tim.
(A gunnel for a boat is a bit like a rib bone for a person and is important for its shape and structure.)

"That just should not be allowed" said Marmaduke who was not used to having rascals about or bad things happening.

"It's not the first time." replied Tim.

"Poor Tim" Yasmin sympathised – "when did it happen before?"

"When you were away last week, Yasmin - on your cruise back from Grapeland. These three came out of the pub, caused trouble and kicked me then."

"That is outrageous!" said Marmaduke. "We must do something about this. We can't have our small friend Tim being kicked by these drunken sailors; we MUST stop them."

"At once" said Robert the Racing Dinghy loudly, "but how?"

"In the olden days" replied Willie the Working Boat, "we would have clapped them in irons overnight and left them out in the cold to sober up." Willie always thought that the old ways were best, and that there had been less trouble years ago when punishment was harsher.

"Shame we can't do that now" said Marmaduke who was cross that Tim the smallest boat had been picked on.
"Hold on a minute" said Kevin the Canvas Canoe. "Did you say last week? Was it Friday last week – the same day as today?"
"Why yes" said Tim, "I suppose it was. Why do you ask?"
"That is interesting" said Kevin.

Something was going through Kevin's mind. The other boats knew that he was working something out.

"Friday is payday for the sailors. I think they come ashore on Friday, go to the pub with their week's wages, spend too much and end up drunk" said Kevin. "It may happen again next Friday, so we could be ready for them when they come next time."

"Ooh what a good idea, Kevin" said Yasmin – "shall we ambush them?"

At that idea the boats got very excited and started talking all at once.

"I have an idea." said Kevin……………………

Over the next week Kevin thought about his idea and dis-cussed the ambush with the other boats. They were going to teach the sailors a lesson they would not forget.

The following Friday came and unusually not all the boats were in their normal places. Both Willie and Marmaduke were back in the water, tied up on two sides of the pontoon. Tim had moved onto a higher rack which was too high to kick at. Yasmin had moved into Marmaduke's position. She could now see the pub up the road and make signals down the road to the pontoon. Her red and green lights had been covered at the front so now only the stern light was uncovered ("stern" means back of the boat). This could only be seen from the pontoon by Marmaduke and Willie.

"Is everyone ready?" said Kevin.
"Yes" they all replied.

They could hear the buzz of people chatting in the pub. The pub lights twinkled out of the windows casting their yellowish lights into the garden outside. But it was dark down towards the water.

They watched and they waited, and they waited and they watched.

From about 10 o'clock, most of the people started leaving the pub.

But the sailors were not to be seen. Where had they gone? Were they still inside? The boats watched and waited. Time ticked by…10.30, 11, 11.30, 12…………

Just as they were all tiring and thinking the sailors must have left by the back door and gone a different way home, the front door of the pub burst open and the three sailors tumbled out.

"It's only midnight and the wretched landlord wants to close" said one drunken sailor.
"It's not fair" said a second.
The third lashed out with his boot, kicking a plant in the pub's front garden.
It was the same three sailors, and they were staggering back down to the pontoon where their motor boat was tied up.

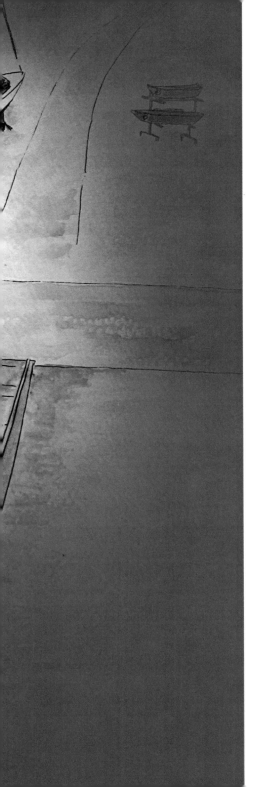

As the sailors left the pub, Yasmin flashed her stern navigation light, on and off. The sailors were unaware that the signal had been made to alert the boats on the water.

Although they could not see the pub, Willie and Marmaduke saw Yasmin's light flash on and off. "It's them" whispered Willie, "Yasmin has signalled that they are leaving the pub and coming this way"

"Are you ready?" murmured Marmaduke.

The sailors came down the path towards the pontoon. One of them lashed out with his boot in the direction of where Tim normally was, but his boot went into empty space.
The drunken sailors staggered on in the dark making their way by the light of the moon.
They stepped up onto the pontoon and walked half way along. Suddenly, Marmaduke's horn sounded, PARP, PARP, PARP. Robert clanged a rope* up against his mast CLANG CLANG CLANG and Yasmin turned on all her lights.

The sailors were surprised by the noise and lights.

*A rope which runs up the mast used for hoisting sails, is called a halyard.

One said to another, "something funny is going on here, quick, let's return to the motor boat." And they started to run down the pontoon.

They were just coming up to a corner when Willie sounded his fog horn
Booooop....................
Booooop......................Booooop.

That startled the sailors who looked over their shoulders to see where the noise was coming from.

Willie said to Marmaduke "NOW!"

And with that Willie and Marmaduke pulled up
a rope which had been lying on the floor
before the corner of the pontoon. The sailors
ran straight into the rope which caught them
around the ankles. They tripped up and over
they went, splash, then splash, and splash, as
each one went into the water.

"Hooray!" shouted the boats.
The sailors slowly pulled themselves out of the
cold water, looking very silly and wet. They got
into their motor boat and sped off into the
moonlit estuary.

To this day they have never returned to be a nuisance to Kevin and his friends at Sandybanks beach. And Tim whose gunnel was cracked, had it repaired in the yard and is now stronger than before.

The End.

Other titles in the series

ISBN number 978-0-9934322-1-7

Mucky Water Mystery

During a night-time trip, Kevin and his boat friends investigate who is responsible for the mess in the Summerwater.

ISBN number 978-0-9934322-0-0

Simon the Speedboat and the SOS

An SOS call breaks the peace in Boatland. Can Kevin and friends rescue Demelza and can Simon the Speedboat go as fast as he says?

More stories to come -
See www.topsails.co.uk for the latest additions